The big guns boom all night.
My head feels like it will explode.
I hate the stink of this place.
I wish I was back in the garden...

OVER THE TOP

The Story of a Soldier

"YOUR COUNTRY NEEDS

YOU"

World War 1 began in the summer of 1914. Britain went to war with Germany.

The men of Britain were asked to fight for their king and country.

Thousands of men signed up.

Many young men wanted to go to the battlefields in France. They thought it would be an adventure.

They could not imagine the horror of the battlefields...

BANG
BOOM

The ground shakes.

My ears feel like they
will explode!

BANG
BOOM

The night sky glows with smoke and fire.
My ears feel like they will explode.

I wish I was back in England.
I wish I was back in the garden.
I wish I could hear a bird sing....

I'm digging.
The sun is warm on my back.
The birds are singing.

I can hear my friend
Harry whistling.
He's planting seeds.

Harry

It is cold and wet in the trenches.

My belly rumbles.
We had bread and stew for supper.
Just one loaf of bread for ten lads.
The bread was hard and dry.
It takes eight days for bread
to get here.

BANG
BOOM

There is icy water in the trenches.

Our boots are filled with it day
and night.

Our feet are burning and rotting.

It's trench foot.
All us lads have got it.

Annie

SURELY YOU WILL
FIGHT FOR YOUR

AND

COME ALONG, BOYS,
BEFORE IT IS TOO LATE

We are sitting by the pond.
The sun is hot on my back.
The water is icy cold on my hot feet.

I give Harry half my bread.
It's sweet and soft.
Annie baked it this morning.

Harry says, "I'm going, Jack.
We should go together."

BANG
BOOM

I hate the stink of this place.
The stink of our lads rotting
in the mud.

I wish I was back in the garden.

I want to smell flowers
and fruit....

Harry is high up the ladder.
He's picking apples.
I'm holding the basket.

Harry says, "We'll go on a ship!
Better to be a soldier than a
gardener, Jack."

I love the smell of the apples.

Tonight, Annie will bake
apple pudding.

BANG BOOM

The big guns boom all night.
Killing the Germans in
their trenches.

Clearing the way for
our lads to attack.

We keep watch.
Some lads try to sleep.
It will soon be time.

We're going over the top.

I will write to Annie.
I get a pencil and paper.

My hands are icy cold.
It's hard to write.

BANG
BOOM

Dear Annie,
All is good here.

I open the door and
Harry is waiting.

Harry says, "Come on, Jack.
We're marching to the coast.
We're off to France, Jack."

Annie tries not to cry.
She says, "Take care,
little brother."

I say, "I'm going to do
my duty, Annie."

Jack
1916

Annie and
Jack 1901

BANG
BOOM

It's getting light.
It will soon be time.
I stamp my icy, burning feet.
I scratch at the lice in my hair.

Dear Annie,

All is good here.

I am keeping fit and well.

My head is filled with pictures.

Sometimes my head feels like it
will explode.

I can't forget that night.
Harry was smiling and singing.
The lads were clapping along.

BANG
BANG
BANG

A sniper, close to our trench.
Harry's body crumpled, and fell
back into the mud.

Blood was pouring from his head.
My best friend was dead.

It's getting light.
It will soon be time.
I finish my letter to Annie.
It will be posted back to England.

The rum is coming around.
A shot of rum for each lad.
A shot of rum to take away the fear.

Then the big guns stop.
It is time.

We are going over the top.

The whistles blow.
I'm climbing out of
the trench.

Running

Deep mud pulls at my boots.
Dead, rotting bodies under
my feet.

Machine
guns
flash

My ears feel like they
will explode.

I have to keep going.

Running and
running.

Machine
guns
flash

Sharp wire tears at my legs.

"Better to be a
soldier than a
gardener, Jack."

Screams all around me.

"Take care,
little brother."

I'm doing my duty, Annie.
I have to keep going.

Dear Annie,

All is good here.

I am keeping fit and well.

I miss the garden.

Are the apples ready for picking?

I am taking care of myself.

I hope to be home soon.

Your loving brother

Jack

OVER THE TOP:
Behind the Story

On the battlefields of Europe during the First World War, both sides dug trenches in which soldiers sheltered, fired their weapons, lived and died.

The trenches were long networks of ditches that armies dug along the front lines of territory they held against the enemy. Soldiers on each side then attacked one another and defended their territory from inside the trenches.

Large weapons, called artillery, provided heavy firepower to support the soldiers in the trenches. These weapons fired large shells and other explosives at enemy positions.

Life in the trenches was miserable, boring, and terrifying. Moments of rest were brief, as enemy artillery attacks could come at any time. These attacks were launched from a great distance away, and were impossible to defend against.

Many of the nine million soldiers killed in the First World War died in the trenches. There, artillery, machine-gun fire, and disease made death a constant presence for soldiers on both sides.

Over the Top

Adding to the danger and terror of trench warfare were the times when soldiers went "over the top". Soldiers leapt over the edge of their trench and rushed into an area known as "No Man's Land". Their mission was to cross this area and attack the enemy trenches facing them.

Sometimes this resulted in hand-to-hand combat with enemy soldiers. Often, soldiers going over the top were met by a storm of enemy machine-gun fire, leading to near-certain death.

Soldiers loading large artillery weapons

Mum and Dad

Mollie

BACK IN THE GARDEN
ON YOUR OWN / WITH A PARTNER / IN A GROUP

In the story, Jack remembers the garden, the birds singing, the apples, and his sister's cooking. If you were forced to spend time away from your home and everyday life, what would you miss the most?

DEAR ANNIE
ON YOUR OWN

The letter Jack writes to his sister, Annie, does not reveal the full horror of his life in the trenches.

Imagine you are Jack. Write a letter home that tells the truth about the terrible things you are experiencing.

Dear Annie,
All is good here.
I am keeping fit and well.
I miss the garden.
Are the apples ready for picking?
I am taking care of myself.
I hope to be home soon.
Your loving brother
Jack

Jack and Harry are characters in a story. Their story, however, is based on what happened to thousands of men who fought during World War One. Discuss with your group how the story and the facts you've learned about the war make you feel. Think about:

- Could you cope with the conditions that Jack describes in the trenches?

- How do you think the soldiers felt as they went over the top and ran towards the enemy's guns?

A SOLDIER'S SONG
ON YOUR OWN / WITH A PARTNER / IN A GROUP

Many powerful poems and songs have been written about war.

Try writing your own poem or the lyrics to a song about the character Jack or another young soldier in WWI. Think about a theme or main idea for your song. Don't be afraid to write down words or partial ideas – they may give you inspiration later!

I die tomorrow

Hell on earth

the boy from the garden

goodbye home

Titles in the
Yesterday's Voices
series

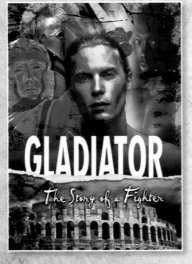

I waited deep below the arena.
Then it was my turn to fight.
Kill or be killed!

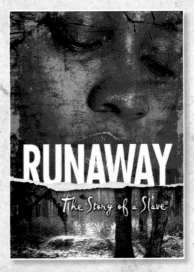

I cannot live as a slave
any longer. Tonight, I will
escape and never go back.

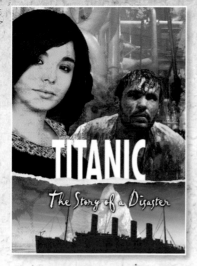

TITANIC
The Story of a Disaster

The ship is sinking into the icy sea. I don't want to die. Someone help us!

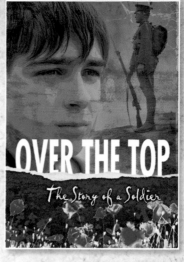

OVER THE TOP
The Story of a Soldier

I'm waiting in the trench. I am so afraid. Tomorrow we go over the top.

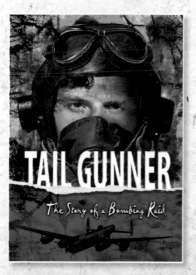

TAIL GUNNER
The Story of a Bombing Raid

Another night. Another bombing raid. Will this night be the one when we don't make it back?

HOLOCAUST
The Story of a Survivor

They took my clothes and shaved my head. I was no longer a human.